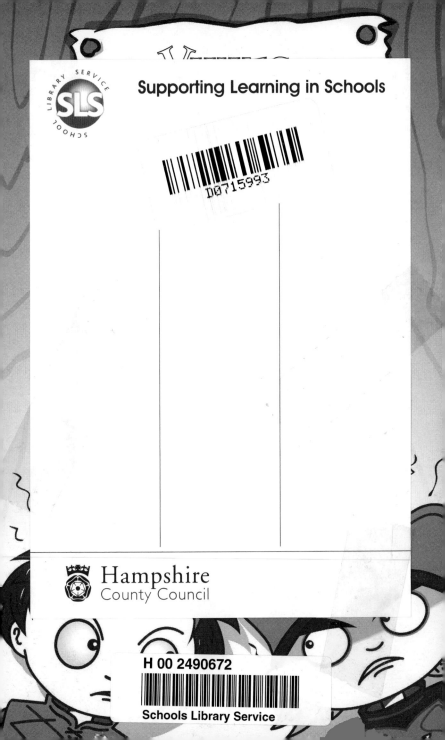

FOR
ANNE LISE

ORCHARD BOOKS
338 Euston Road, London NW1 3BH
Orchard Books Australia
Level 17/207 Kent St, Sydney, NSW 2000

ISBN 978 1 84616 717 1 (hardback)
ISBN 978 1 84616 725 6 (paperback)

Text and illustrations © Shoo Rayner 2008

A CIP catalogue record for this book is available from the British Library.

1 3 5 7 9 10 8 6 4 2 (hardback)
1 3 5 7 9 10 8 6 4 2 (paperback)

Printed in Great Britain

Orchard Books is a division of Hachette Children's Books,
an Hachette Livre UK company.

www.hachettelivre.co.uk

VIKING VIK

AND THE WOLVES

SHOO RAYNER

ORCHARD BOOKS

"Hail to the mighty
ocean!" Vik yelled
from the top of a huge
boulder. He held his fist
high, saluting the sea
which glittered far
below him. "I wish
I could be sailing out
there," he sighed.

"Maybe next year,"
said Freya.

Wulf leapt on the rock and poked Vik in the ribs. "You'd be useless on a Longship," he snarled. "Anyway, Dad's taking *me* next year."

"Dad said he'd take one of you," Freya corrected. "He said he'd take whoever was the most help to Mum."

Wulf shoved Vik hard in the chest. "He won't need a weakling jellyfish like Vik!" Vik fought to keep his balance, but he tripped and crashed onto the springy mountain grass.

Wulf jumped on top of him and in seconds they were rolling around, scrapping and fighting. Vik's dog, Flek, snapped and barked, adding to the chaos.

"You two are useless," Freya fumed. "Dad should take *me* with him."

The two boys stopped fighting, stared at Freya in amazement and collapsed into fits of laughter.

"But you're a girl!" they taunted. "Girls are no use on Longships!"

Yes — it was just
another normal day
looking after the goats
on the high pasture
above Snekkevik.

GOATHERDING

In summer the goats are taken
up to the mountain meadows
to eat the grass.

The goat girls
turn the milk
into cheese
to eat in
the winter.

The grass at the bottom of the
mountain is grown to make
hay to feed the goats in winter.

Why are they
goat girls,
not boys?

Because the
boys are away,
raiding in the
Longships.

As night fell, they huddled round the campfire. Vik stared into the flames. "This is the most boring job in the world. All we do is watch the goats all day, and then we have to sleep out here and watch them through the night! I don't half miss my little bed."

"At least the summer nights aren't really dark," said Freya, looking up at the stars.

"I saw Greeneyes the wolf last night," said Vik. "He was on the other side of the fiord and half his pack were with him. He was watching us."

Freya's eyes grew large and round. "You should have woken us up!"

"It was my turn
to keep watch,"
Vik said proudly.
"I waved a burning
stick at them. They
soon went away."

Wulf laughed.
"You're making it
up! Greeneyes is
just an old story.
Wolves don't have
green eyes."

"I know what I saw,"
Vik said firmly.
"The moon was bright
and his eyes glittered
like emeralds."

That night, Wulf took first turn on
watch, so Vik lay down on the grass
and stared up at the dark blue sky.
Flek snuggled up next to him.

The brilliant, shining stars made
shapes in Vik's imagination. He saw
Thor, the mighty god of war, and
plenty of wolves, too. As his eyes closed
and sleep came over him, one bright
star winked at him – Greeneyes!

THE MIDNIGHT SUN

In summer in the far north, the days are so long that the sun hardly sets. This is because the Earth is tilted as it spins.

Snekkevik

Summer

The Vikings believe that the sun and moon are chariots that are chased across the sky by wolves. In the summer, the sun takes the lead from the moon.

In his dream, Vik suddenly heard a voice very close to his ear: "Wolves! Greeneyes!"

Vik woke instantly, grabbed his wooden sword and sprang into action, ready to fight off the vicious wolf-attack. Flek stood firm by his side, growling and baring his teeth.

But Freya was sleeping peacefully and
the goats were dozing quietly all around
him. There was no sign of any wolves at
all. Wulf rolled on the ground, clutching
his sides, laughing his head off!

"Ha! Ha! Ha! Look at the mighty warrior!" Tears streamed down Wulf's face.

"You said there were wolves!" Vik snapped back, angrily.

"You must have been dreaming!"
Wulf said, innocently. "But since
you're wide awake now," he sneered,
"you can take over the guard duty."

Wulf snuggled under his blanket and fell asleep in an instant – a wicked grin slid across his face.

"I might have been dreaming of wolves," Vik muttered under his breath, "but I didn't dream Wulf's alarm call!"

The next day, Vik's head felt muzzy from lack of sleep. They'd taken the goats to their mother's hut for milking and now they were in a new meadow.

The goats were eating grass, Freya was picking flowers and Wulf, with nothing else to do, was teasing Vik.

"Greeneyes! You'll be dreaming that Dad will pick you to go on the Longship, next."

Vik wasn't going to let Wulf wind him up. He busied himself collecting firewood for their camp.

That night, the very same thing happened. As Vik slept and dreamt that he was a famous warrior, he heard a voice close to his ear: "Wolves! Greeneyes!"

"Wolves! Greeneyes!"

Once again, Vik sprang into action.

Once again, Wulf bent over in fits of laughter. "Ha! Ha! You've been dreaming again!"

And once again, Vik took over the watch. As the sun rose slowly in the sky, he stirred deep, dark thoughts in his mind.

Vik glared at the sleeping Wulf. "It wasn't a dream," he muttered. "Just wait…I'll get even!"

Freya woke early.
Vik told her what
he'd been thinking.
"Oh dear!" she
sighed. "Will you two
never be friends?"

The next night Vik's
plan was ready...

THE WOLVES

Wolves roam the mountains
and forests of Snekkevik.

They live and hunt in packs.

Greeneyes is the leader of his pack.
Some people don't believe he's real.
Maybe he's a ghost wolf!

"I'll take first watch tonight," Vik announced.

Wulf was suspicious. "I'll play you Bones for it."

Vik stood his ground.
"No! It's my turn."

Wulf couldn't argue with that. He'd done the first watch for the last two nights. "OK," he said, warily. "But don't wake me until dawn."

As the short night began, the
sun dipped below the sea and
a huge moon rose into the sky.
Wulf was soon fast asleep and
snoring under his fur blanket.
"Freya, wake up!"
Vik whispered. "Let's go!"

HOW TO PLAY BONES

You need five
knucklebones from
a sheep or goat, and
a leather ball or stone.

Throw the ball in the air and catch it
with one hand. When the ball is in the
air, pick up a knucklebone with the
other hand. When you have picked up
all the bones, change hands.

The winner is the person who picks
up the most knucklebones.

Quietly, they gathered their things, rounded up the goats and led them to a hidden ravine at the bottom of the meadow.

"Stay here and look after the goats," Vik told Freya. "Come on Flek, we've got work to do."

Vik and Flek climbed a rocky
crag above the camp. Vik took
aim and threw some pebbles at
Wulf's sleeping hulk.

"Bull's-eye!" Vik cheered, as a pebble
bounced off Wulf's head. Wulf leapt to
his feet. His fists were clenched, ready
for mortal combat.

Hiding behind the rock, Vik grabbed
Flek and tickled his tummy.

There was nothing Flek liked better than having his tummy tickled. He threw his head back and howled with joy. The eerie noise echoed around the mountains, and soon Flek sounded like a whole pack of wolves!

YOWWWL

FLEK'S FIVE
FAVOURITE THINGS

1. Sniffing dog poo!

 2. Sniffing rocks
that other dogs
have weed on.

3. Eating boiled sheep's
brains with carrots.

4. Chasing sticks.

5. Having
his tummy
tickled.

Wulf had woken with a pain in his head. He sensed he was all alone.

Where were Vik and Freya?

YOOOWWLLL

Where were Flek and the goats?

And what was that terrible noise?

Wulf stared at the craggy rocks above him. A hideous shape stood silhouetted against the huge, silver moon. The beast howled to the star-filled sky and was answered by others all around. Wulf was surrounded!

He turned and fled down the valley, tripping and falling over the moonlit shadows.

When Wulf returned later, a scene of peace and serenity met his eyes. He'd brought his mother and the frightened goat girls with him to see if the wolves had left anything alive.

But there was Vik, on guard, alert and brave with his faithful dog at his side. Freya slept by the glowing fire while the goats dozed in their strange, goaty way.

"Where are the wolves?" Mum demanded.

"Wolves?" Vik asked, sweetly. "There are no wolves here. Wulf must have had a bad dream.

"He woke up, shouting 'Greeneyes!', and ran off into the dark. I couldn't leave the goats while I was on duty – I didn't know what to do. I'm so glad you're safe, Wulf!"

"But –" Wulf looked confused. He scratched his head. "Ow! But – no one was here when I woke up. The goats had gone. I saw a wolf. I heard them all howling."

Vik gave Wulf a tender look. "You must have been dreaming," he explained gently, as if he were talking to a three-year-old. "Oh! Is that the sun? I think it's your turn to guard the goats now."

Mum gave Wulf a lecture about
looking after the goats and told him not
to be so stupid. "And stop listening to
those old tales of Greeneyes the Wolf!"
she yelled, as she led the goat girls back
to their hut.

"Yes, Mum," Wulf mumbled, sulkily.

Vik snuggled down to sleep. He put his arm around Flek, gave him a big hug and tickled his tummy.

"Ow-ow-owwwww!" Flek howled.

"Shhh!" Vik giggled under his blanket. "Be quiet, Flek! Some of us are trying to sleep!"

SHOO RAYNER

All priced at £3.99

The Viking Vik stories are available from all good bookshops,
or can be ordered direct from the publisher:
Orchard Books, PO BOX 29, Douglas IM99 1BQ
Credit card orders please telephone 01624 836000
or fax 01624 837033 or visit our internet site: www.orchardbooks.co.uk
or e-mail: bookshop@enterprise.net for details.

To order please quote title, author and ISBN
and your full name and address.
Cheques and postal orders should be made payable to 'Bookpost plc.'
Postage and packing is FREE within the UK
(overseas customers should add £2.00 per book).

Prices and availability are subject to change.